THE
WEE
MOOSE

by Gina Bell-Zano
illustrated by Enrico Arno

Parents' Magazine Press
A Division of Parents' Magazine Enterprises, Inc.
New York

It was a lovely spring day–
a perfect day for playing in the hay in the barn.

A small mouse was doing just that. He was hav-
ing fun even though he had nobody to play with.

Suddenly, he heard the footsteps of Farmer MacGuff who owned the farm where the small mouse lived.

The small mouse looked around for a safe place to hide. He was so frightened his whiskers trembled. But the farmer saw him first.

"Do not be afraid," said the farmer in a kind voice. "I would never harm a wee moose like you."

He turned his back on the small mouse and went on with his work.

The small mouse sat very still. He was thinking about what the farmer had said. "So," he said to himself, "I am a wee moose, am I? Now I wonder what that is. I must look for another wee moose, and then I'll know. Maybe I'll even find a friend."

He crept quietly out of the barn and looked all around. There were other animals about.

He went up to a cow, who was busy eating grass. "Pardon me," he shouted loudly, for the cow was very large and very high. "Are you a moose?"

"Why, no, indeed," said the cow, "I am a cow."

"Well," said the small mouse, "I am a moose and I'd like to meet another moose."

"You, a moose?" said the cow. She was so surprised that she stopped eating.

"Well, I'm a wee moose," said the small mouse.

"Oh, dear," said the cow, "where did you get that idea?"

"Farmer MacGuff told me so himself," the small mouse said proudly.

The cow didn't know what to say. Farmer MacGuff was never wrong. When she had chewed some more grass, she said, "Why don't you ask the horse? He gets around more than I do. He may know where to find a moose."

"Where is he?" shouted the small mouse.

"Right over there, near the fence," said the cow.

"Thank you," said the small mouse, and he hurried over to the horse.

He had to shout even louder because the horse was larger and even higher than the cow. "Pardon me," he shouted, "I'm looking for a moose."

"There are none on a farm," said the horse, kindly. "They live in the woods."

"Thank you," shouted the small mouse. "I'd like to find one, for I am a wee moose myself."

"You are? Who told you that?" asked the horse.

"Farmer MacGuff told me that himself," the small mouse said proudly.

The horse didn't know what to say. Farmer MacGuff was never wrong. "Well, try the woods," he finally said.

"Thank you again," said the small mouse, hurrying off. He ran and scampered until he came to the woods.

He looked all around. There was not another animal, small or large, in sight. There were only trees, and some wild flowers, and a large brook. He looked toward the brook. The water was sparkling in the sunlight. He felt thirsty. He thought a cool drink of water would be fine. He scampered over to the edge of the brook and took a long, cool drink.

Just then, a very large animal came up to the
brook and began to drink.

"Pardon me," shouted the small mouse, and
he had to shout very loudly indeed, for this animal
was even larger and higher than the horse. "Pardon me, do you know where I can find a moose?"
he asked.

The large animal lowered his head. "I am a
moose," he said very softly.

"Well, so am I," said the small mouse. "I am a wee moose."

"Who told you that?" asked the moose.

"Why Farmer MacGuff told me so himself," said the small mouse proudly.

"Then I'm afraid that Farmer MacGuff has made a mistake. Come, little thing, look into the brook with me. See if you look like me."

"Well, of course," said the small mouse, "I know I'm much smaller, but I'm a wee one of you."

Side by side they stood at the edge of the brook and looked into the clear water.

There were large horns on the top of the moose's head. The small mouse touched the top of his head with his paw. No horns, not even tiny ones, were there. The moose had a large, flat face. The mouse's was small and pointed. The moose had a short ball of fur for a tail. The mouse had a long, thin one, like a string.

"I guess Farmer MacGuff is wrong at last," said the mouse. "I'm not a moose, not even a wee one." And his little beady eyes filled with little shiny tears.

The moose shook his head in sympathy. Then he said, "Look, why don't you go to see the Wise Old Owl? He'll be able to explain things to you. He always knows the answers."

"Thank you. I'm sorry I'm not one of you—even a wee one of you. You are a handsome animal," said the small mouse.

He hurried on until he came to the tree house of the Wise Old Owl. He knocked at the door. The Wise Old Owl was polite, as always. "How do you do. What can I do for you?" he said.

"Oh, Mr. Owl, I have a problem. I need some advice," said the small mouse.

"Of course you do," said the Wise Old Owl, "that's the only time anyone comes to see me."

"Am I a wee moose?" asked the small mouse. "Am I?"

"No," said the Wise Old Owl. "Who told you that?"

"Farmer MacGuff told me so himself," said the small mouse. "With his own mouth he told me that I was a wee moose."

"I'm afraid you didn't understand him," said the Wise Old Owl. "You see, Farmer MacGuff comes from Scotland. That's a land far away, and the people who live there speak differently from the people who live here. When he said you were a wee moose, he meant mouse, but that's the way they talk in Scotland. Is that clear to you?"

"Yes," said the small mouse, in a small voice, "very clear. But I do wish I knew a wee mouse like me. I get tired of being alone all the time."

"Oh," said the Wise Old Owl, "I can fix that." He gave a quick kind of whistle and a very small mouse crept out from behind the tree. "This is a wee mouse," said the Wise Old Owl. "Her name is Fifi. She lives around here. Be friends." The Wise Old Owl went back into his tree house and closed the door. He was still sleepy.

The two mice looked at each other. The small mouse smiled and his whiskers twitched. Fifi smiled, too.

Then the small mouse said, "Fifi, would you like to come and live on my farm? There is plenty of food, and it's warm in the winter and cool in the summer. I do get so lonely."

"All right," said Fifi, "I don't mind if I do. I get lonely, too."

So the little mice went back to the farm together. They became the very best of friends.

And the small mouse was quite pleased that he was not, after all, a wee moose, for then he would never have found anyone as wonderful as Fifi to make him happy.